32-

Infectious Disease Prevention: Protecting Public Health

Carla Mooney

ReferencePoint Press

San Diego, CA

About the Author

Carla Mooney is the author of many books for young adults and children. She lives in Pittsburgh, Pennsylvania, with her husband and three children.

For more information, contact:
ReferencePoint Press, Inc.
PO Box 27779
San Diego, CA 92198
www.ReferencePointPress.com

Picture Credits:
Cover: aijohn784/Depositphotos
5: Associated Press
10: Shutterstock.com
12: BSIP/Newscom
17: Associated Press
20: imageBROKER/Florian Kopp/Newscom
23: iStock
27: Associated Press
30: Shutterstock.com
34: iStock
38: Shutterstock.com
40: Associated Press
45: iStock
50: Associated Press
53: iStock
56: Associated Press

DEC 0 1 2021

LIBRARY OF CONGRESS CATALOGING-IN-PUBLICATION DATA

Names: Mooney, Carla, 1970- author.
Title: Infectious disease prevention : protecting public health / by Carla Mooney.
Description: San Diego, CA : ReferencePoint Press, Inc., 2022. | Series: Understanding infectious diseases | Includes bibliographical references and index.
Identifiers: LCCN 2021013117 (print) | LCCN 2021013118 (ebook) | ISBN 9781678201586 (library binding) | ISBN 9781678201593 (ebook)
Subjects: LCSH: Health--Juvenile literature. | Medicine, Preventive--Juvenile literature. | Vaccination--Juvenile literature.
Classification: LCC RA777 .M673 2022 (print) | LCC RA777 (ebook) | DDC 614.4--dc23
LC record available at https://lccn.loc.gov/2021013117
LC ebook record available at https://lccn.loc.gov/2021013118

CONTENTS

Preventing Outbreaks Worldwide

In May 2015 health officials in Brazil reported multiple confirmed cases of Zika fever in the country's northeastern region. Zika fever is an infectious disease caused by the Zika virus and is primarily spread by the bite of aedes mosquitoes. Most people infected with Zika do not experience any symptoms, while others experience mild symptoms such as fever, rash, headache, muscle and joint pain, and general fatigue.

In some cases, Zika infections can become severe. Some infected adults and children experience neurological complications such as Guillain-Barré syndrome, a condition in which a person's immune system attacks the body's peripheral nerves. For pregnant women, a Zika infection can cause complications such as miscarriage and preterm birth.

Within months of the first reported cases, Zika spread through South and Central America. In January 2016 the Pan American Health Organization reported that the Zika virus had spread to eighteen countries and territories in the Americas.

During this time, doctors noticed a disturbing trend. Thousands of babies born in Brazil had brain abnormalities and congenital disabilities. Many babies were born with microcephaly, a rare condition in which a baby is born with a smaller-than-normal head or the baby's head stops growing shortly after birth, leading to physical and learning disabilities. The medical community noted a factor the babies had in common: their mothers had been infected with the Zika virus during pregnancy.

It was the first time that a virus spread by mosquitoes was linked to severe birth defects. By February 2016 the World Health Organization (WHO) declared the Zika virus an international public health emergency. "I am now declaring that the recent cluster of microcephaly and other neurological abnormalities reported in Latin America . . . constitutes a public health emergency of international concern,"[1] stated Margaret Chan, WHO director general, at a press conference. She emphasized the need to protect pregnant women from Zika and control the virus's mosquito-borne spread.

After months of studies, the Centers for Disease Control and Prevention (CDC) confirmed the link between Zika infection during pregnancy and microcephaly in infants. "There is no longer any doubt that Zika causes microcephaly," announced

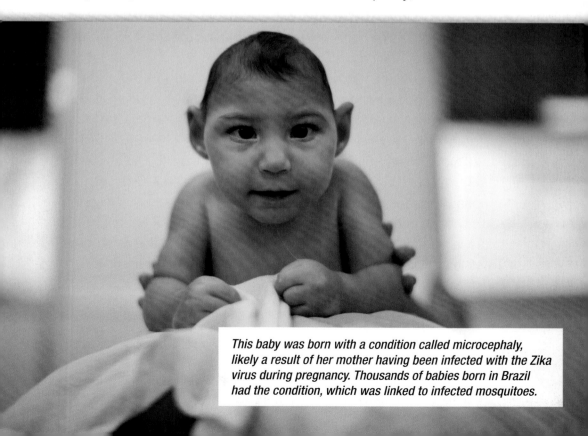

This baby was born with a condition called microcephaly, likely a result of her mother having been infected with the Zika virus during pregnancy. Thousands of babies born in Brazil had the condition, which was linked to infected mosquitoes.

CDC director Dr. Thomas R. Frieden. "Never before in history has there been a situation where a bite from a mosquito can result in a devastating malformation."[2]

Public Health Officials Respond

The WHO, along with local and national public health officials, jumped into action to detect and confirm cases of Zika virus infection and treat people who had contracted the disease. They helped local laboratories acquire the technology and personnel needed to test for the virus in local communities quickly. They set up surveillance of Zika cases to track where the virus was spreading and monitor severe cases and complications.

The WHO consulted with medical and infectious disease experts to prepare guidelines for local medical professionals on how to care for and monitor those infected with the Zika virus. They provided medicines for patients and laboratory supplies for diagnostic testing.

The WHO and public health officials also worked to prevent future Zika outbreaks. They worked with national and local officials to find and eliminate mosquito breeding grounds. They also warned communities and at-risk individuals, especially pregnant women, to protect themselves against mosquito bites by using mosquito repellent and wearing long-sleeve tops and long pants. They also advised pregnant women to avoid traveling to areas affected by the Zika virus.

In November 2016 the WHO declared that the Zika global health emergency had ended but emphasized that Zika was an infectious disease that should still be taken seriously. Although the immediate crisis was over, the threat from the Zika infectious disease remained. Dr. Jeremy Farrar, director of the Wellcome Trust, a London-based health research foundation, explained:

> Zika has once again exposed the world's vulnerability to emerging infectious diseases and the devastation they can unleash. Alongside the emergency response that

Zika necessitates, we must put in place the permanent reforms, health systems strengthening and proactive research agenda that are needed to make the global health system more resilient to the threat of future pandemics.[3]

The Spread of Infectious Diseases

Infectious diseases like Zika can spread quickly through a community and beyond. These diseases are caused by microorganisms such as viruses, bacteria, fungi, and parasites. Some infectious diseases spread by person-to-person contact, while others spread through contaminated food or water or by contact with an infectious insect or animal.

Throughout the world, the threat of infectious disease is high. Microorganisms that cause these diseases adapt and reproduce quickly. As they adapt, they can change how they spread and develop resistance to drugs used to treat and prevent infection. Also, new infectious diseases are emerging more quickly than ever. Since the 1970s, scientists have discovered about forty new infectious diseases.

microorganisms

Microscopic organisms such as bacteria, viruses, parasites, and fungi

Today it is easier for people to travel more often and for greater distances. According to the CDC, an infectious disease can travel from a remote village on one continent to major cities worldwide in only thirty-six hours. As a result, infectious diseases, both new and recurring, can spread rapidly and trigger global epidemics—or pandemics.

Protecting People and Communities

Infectious diseases are one of the leading causes of death around the world. According to the WHO, three of the top ten causes of death worldwide in 2019 were infectious diseases. For poor countries, infectious diseases are even more deadly. Six of the top ten causes of death in low-income countries in 2019 were infectious diseases.

Public health systems protect people and communities by preventing disease, including infectious disease, and promoting health. They monitor the health of a community to detect infectious disease outbreaks quickly. When they detect an infectious disease outbreak, public health professionals work quickly to gather and analyze data to determine the cause of the outbreak and decide what actions to take to control it.

Public health professionals also prevent infections by developing and promoting vaccines, reducing the sources of infectious diseases, and isolating and treating infected people to prevent further disease spread. They develop community education programs to encourage people to change their behavior to reduce infectious disease risk. Through these efforts, public health systems defend the public against infectious diseases worldwide.

CHAPTER ONE

Foodborne Diseases

During the summer of 2015, several people across multiple states in America became ill with salmonella, a bacterial disease commonly spread by eating or drinking contaminated food or water. People infected with salmonella typically experience symptoms of diarrhea, stomach cramps, and fever about twelve to seventy-two hours after they eat contaminated food. To discover the outbreak's source, state and local public health officials interviewed the people who were ill. They asked about the foods the ill people had eaten in the week before they got sick. Interviewers found that 391 of 519 people interviewed (75 percent) reported eating cucumbers recently. This percentage was significantly higher than the percentage of healthy people surveyed who said they ate cucumbers in the past week (47 percent).

As public health officials analyzed the data from the ill people, they identified several illness clusters. An illness cluster occurs when two or more people who do not live together report eating at the same restaurant, attending the same event, or shopping at the same grocery store in the week before becoming sick. Illness clusters provide important clues to investigators. If several people become ill after eating at the same restaurant or shopping at the same store, there is a good chance that the contaminated food was eaten or sold there. In this salmonella investigation, public health officials discovered eleven illness clusters in seven states. In each cluster, investigators found that all of the ill people had eaten cucumbers.

As the investigation increasingly pointed to cucumbers as the source of the salmonella bacteria, health departments collected and tested cucumbers from stores and restaurants near the illness clusters. They isolated the cucumbers that carried the outbreak strain called *Salmonella* Poona. Next, investigators traced the contaminated cucumbers back to a distributor in San Diego, California, Andrew & Williamson Fresh Produce. At the distributor's facility, investigators tested cucumbers on-site. They discovered that some cucumbers imported from Mexico were contaminated with the same strain of salmonella. Genetic analysis found that the salmonella bacteria from the ill people and from the contaminated cucumbers were closely related. It was another piece of evidence pointing to the cucumbers from this facility as the outbreak's source.

In 2015 cucumbers like these were contaminated with salmonella, resulting in hundreds of people across seven states falling ill.

To protect more people from getting sick, Andrew & Williamson Fresh Produce recalled all cucumbers imported from Mexico in September 2015. The company advised customers to either return the cucumbers or throw them away. "The safety and welfare of consumers is the highest priority for our company," said company president Fred Williamson in a statement. "We are taking all precautions possible to prevent further consumption of this product."[4]

According to the CDC, the 2015 salmonella outbreak linked to Mexican cucumbers sickened 907 people across forty states. Most of those infected recovered from the illness. However, not everyone was so lucky. About 28 percent of those infected required hospitalization, and six people died from the infection. Yet public health officials' quick action to find the outbreak's source and warn the public prevented many more people from becoming ill.

Foodborne Disease: A Common Problem

Foodborne infectious diseases like the one caused by salmonella are a common public health problem. Many foodborne illnesses occur when a person eats or drinks food contaminated with pathogens, the bacteria, viruses, or other microorganisms that can cause disease. A person infected with a foodborne pathogen may experience fever, nausea, vomiting, stomach cramps, diarrhea, and other gastrointestinal problems. While some people experience mild symptoms, others can become very ill and even die.

pathogens

Microorganisms that are capable of causing disease

According to CDC estimates, every year, one in six Americans gets sick from eating or drinking contaminated foods or beverages. Of those, approximately 128,000 become sick enough to be hospitalized, and about 3,000 die. Anyone can get a foodborne infection, but people with weakened immune systems, pregnant women, young children, and the elderly have a higher risk of experiencing more severe illness.

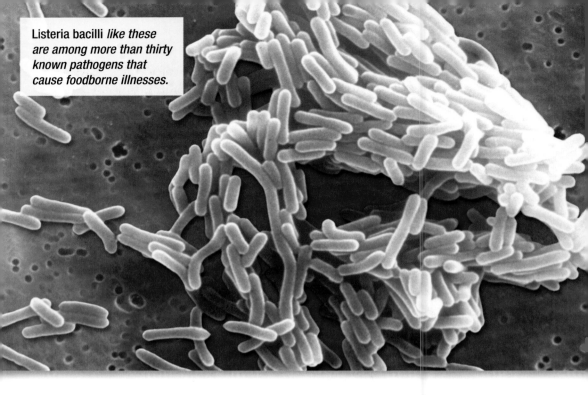

Listeria bacilli *like these are among more than thirty known pathogens that cause foodborne illnesses.*

Currently, there are more than thirty known pathogens that cause foodborne illnesses. Some of the most common are bacteria such as salmonella, listeria, or E. coli. Others are viruses such as norovirus or hepatitis A. Sometimes public health officials can identify the specific pathogen that causes a foodborne illness. Other times an unidentified agent causes a person to get sick. These unknown agents could be microbes, chemicals, or other substances in food and drink that have not yet been identified.

Detecting an Outbreak

Public health systems track illnesses caused by foodborne pathogens so that they can quickly detect a potential outbreak. They review formal health care reports, surveillance systems, and informal reports, such as calls to the local public health department. When these reports show a sudden spike in the number of people contracting a foodborne illness in the same area within the same period, investigators take action. If investigators determine that the sick people have something in common—a food they ate or restaurant they visited—which explains why they all got sick, the group of illnesses becomes an outbreak.

Once public health officials have detected an outbreak of foodborne illness, they attempt to find everyone who has become sick. Finding all related cases helps public health officials better understand the size and severity of an outbreak. To find additional cases, investigators review surveillance reports. They talk to clinical and laboratory professionals and ask them to report suspected cases as soon as possible. They also review emergency room records for illnesses that appear similar to the outbreak. They question groups of people who may have been exposed to the infectious disease to determine whether any have become sick. Investigators also talk to health officials in surrounding areas to see whether they have noticed any illnesses that might be similar or related to the outbreak.

Investigators track an outbreak using a graph called an epidemic curve. This graph tracks the number of illnesses over time. The epidemic curve pattern helps investigators determine whether the sick people were exposed to the foodborne disease over a

Outbreak Investigation Team

When a foodborne outbreak occurs, a team of professionals works together to gather information, find the source, and prevent further illness. Typically, the group includes epidemiologists, who are trained to study diseases in a population. Other team members are microbiologists, scientists who study samples and pathogens in laboratories. Environmental health specialists are part of the investigation and inspect restaurants to ensure they serve safe food. Regulatory compliance officers and inspectors visit restaurants, food distributors, and food processors to verify that all food safety laws are being followed and identify where food safety procedures may have broken down. Health communication specialists prepare announcements to the public about potential outbreaks and food safety tips. All of these professionals work together to keep the public safe from foodborne infectious diseases.

short or long period. Investigators also mark where ill people live so they can see whether and how the outbreak is spreading.

Look for the Source

In an outbreak investigation, public health officials gather information about sick people, where they live, when they got ill, and their symptoms. They research past outbreaks with similar symptoms or pathogens. They search for contacts with other sick people. With all of this data, investigators look for patterns and connections that might help them identify the foodborne outbreak source. They also take specimens from those who are sick. Laboratory testing of samples can identify the type of pathogen causing the person's illness.

Often, investigators gather essential information through interviews with those who are sick. Investigators will ask the ill people what they ate and where they went in the days before they got ill. These interviews help investigators determine whether there is a particular food, ingredient, or other exposure that the infected people have in common. With this information, they can create a short list of foods and drinks that the ill people have in common.

Using all of this data, public health officials make a hypothesis, or possible explanation, for the foodborne outbreak source. They test and analyze food items taken from a sick person's home, grocery store, restaurant, or other location to identify the specific pathogen that caused the illness. Testing can also identify a pathogen's specific deoxyribonucleic acid (DNA) fingerprint.

DNA fingerprint

Unique, identifying patterns in the DNA of an individual organism

Scientists test different foods, searching for pathogens with the same DNA fingerprint found in samples from a sick person. Finding a match provides strong evidence of a likely infection source.

Food contamination can occur anywhere in the food production chain. Food can become contaminated during production or processing, transportation and handling, and preparation before

Linking Cases with PulseNet

Public health officials rely on PulseNet, a national laboratory network, to fully iden-tify foodborne disease outbreaks. PulseNet consists of eighty-three public health and food regulatory laboratories. Individual labs upload DNA fingerprints of patho-gens that are making people sick in their area to PulseNet. The network uses the DNA fingerprints to connect groups of illnesses caused by the same contaminated food or the same disease-causing microorganisms. If the pathogens from two sep-arate cases have similar DNA fingerprints, they are likely related. PulseNet allows public health officials to detect thousands of local and multistate outbreaks that could otherwise be missed.

serving. Public health officials use traceback investigations to de-termine where and when contamination occurred. Investigators trace a food's movement from a sick person back to restaurants, stores, distributors, processors, and producers. They search for a common point between sick people or places where contami-nation may have happened. Investigators may decide to perform environmental assessments at any food production facilities, stores, or restaurants to discover any safety risks that may have led to food contamination.

Control the Outbreak

Once public health officials have identified the source of an out-break, they take action to protect the public from further infec-tions. If contaminated food remains in stores, restaurants, or home pantries, more people may become ill. There are several measures public health officials can take to control a foodborne outbreak. They may order food facilities to be cleaned and disin-fected. Public health officials may temporarily close a restaurant or processing plant until they are sure the pathogen is no longer present. They may issue a recall of potentially contaminated foods and instruct consumers to throw away or return any question-able food in their homes. To prevent foodborne outbreaks, public health systems also educate citizens about safe cooking procedures such as cooking raw foods to the proper temperature. Public health officials choose which control measures to use based on the specific details of each outbreak. As they learn more during an investigation, they may change control measures and messages to the public.

As long as contaminated food remains in homes and stores, the risk of illness remains. Therefore, timely communication with the public is one of the most important measures to control an outbreak and prevent further infection. When a clear link between illness and contaminated food is established, public health officials quickly warn consumers about the risk of eating or drinking potentially contaminated food. Often, they recommend returning or disposing of the food immediately.

When the number of new cases drops back to normal levels, a foodborne outbreak ends. Although the outbreak is over, the work continues. Public health professionals continue surveillance to monitor cases for several weeks. If cases rise again, the investigation resumes.

Investigating a Cyclospora Outbreak

In 2020 the CDC, the US Food and Drug Administration (FDA), and state public health officials investigated an outbreak of cyclospora infections in several states. Cyclospora is a one-celled parasite that spreads when people consume contaminated water or food. People infected with cyclospora typically report symptoms such as diarrhea, stomach cramps, gas, nausea, low fever, and fatigue.

In the 2020 outbreak, public health officials interviewed the ill people and asked them about the foods they ate, places visited, and other exposures in the two weeks before becoming sick. Many of those infected reported eating bagged salad mixes that contained iceberg lettuce, carrots, and red cabbage. They purchased the bagged salad mixes from several grocery stores, including Aldi, Hy-Vee, Jewel-Osco, and Walmart. The stores sold

An outbreak of cyclospora in 2020 was traced to contamination in a facility in Illinois, where a salad mixture like this one was packaged.

the bagged salads under the Fresh Express brand or a private store label brand.

The FDA's traceback investigation tracked the bagged salad mixes from the grocery stores back to a common producer. The investigators suspected that the Fresh Express production facility in Streamwood, Illinois, was the likely source of the contaminated salad. The FDA opened an investigation of the production facility to determine which ingredient or ingredients in the bagged salad mix was the source of the cyclospora illnesses.

In June 2020 the CDC and FDA issued safety alerts to consumers in several midwestern states to avoid eating bagged salads sold at select stores. "The FDA is working with the companies to determine the source of the products, but in the meantime, we are issuing a public warning to consumers to avoid the identified products to prevent additional infections,"[5] Frank Yiannas, FDA deputy commissioner for food policy and response, said in a statement.

On June 27, 2020, Fresh Express issued a voluntary recall of salad mixes produced at the Streamwood production facility that included iceberg lettuce, red cabbage, or carrots. "Our immediate thoughts and concern are for those consumers who have become ill due to the outbreak," Fresh Express said in a statement. "Out of an abundance of caution, we have issued a voluntary recall of both branded and private label salad products that were produced at the Streamwood facility and contain those ingredients."[6]

By September 25, 2020, the CDC announced that the cyclospora outbreak had ended. As of September 23, 2020, confirmed cases of cyclospora infections linked to the outbreak affected 701 people across fourteen states. No deaths were linked to the outbreak.

Not every foodborne illness outbreak is solved. Sometimes an outbreak ends before public health investigators can identify the source of the illness. Public health officials are working on new ways to solve outbreaks faster in order to protect the public from foodborne diseases more effectively.

CHAPTER TWO

Waterborne Diseases

In 2019 an area in northern Cameroon reported a troubling increase in cholera cases. "The town of Pitoa has reported a dozen cases of cholera, including three deaths, in a short period—and these cases do not seem to be related to each other. The situation is particularly worrying, because it means that cholera has spread in the community,"[7] says Justin Eyong, an epidemiologist with Doctors Without Borders, an international humanitarian medical organization.

Cholera is a serious and highly contagious waterborne disease caused by drinking water or eating food contaminated with the *Vibrio cholerae* bacterium. These bacteria are typically found in water contaminated by an infected person's feces or vomit. Some people infected with cholera can experience watery diarrhea and vomiting. If untreated, cholera can lead to severe dehydration or death.

In Cameroon cholera outbreaks occur regularly. The region's rainy season increases the risk of contaminated water mixing with drinking water sources. Additionally, conflicts in the area have forced people to move, weakened existing sanitation systems, and lowered hygiene practices. All of these factors make it easier for cholera to spread through a community.

In response to the 2019 outbreak, local health officials in Cameroon opened an investigation by interviewing people

Public health officials in Cameroon helped educate children about how basic hygiene practices such as handwashing can prevent outbreaks of diseases like cholera.

who showed cholera infection symptoms about their recent diet, movements, and other activities. "It was found that almost half of the cases had contact with dubious water sources: probably contaminated water used to wash clothes or dishes, or wells dug near contaminated latrines,"[8] says Eyong. Through these interviews, investigators were able to identify potentially contaminated water sources. "We are also considering the disinfection of some water sources and will make a call for improved access to clean drinking water in the long term,"[9] says Alphonse Elogo, a Doctors Without Borders water and sanitation specialist.

The epidemiological investigation helped public health officials create a targeted response to the outbreak. The response included disinfecting contaminated water sources, educating the community on hygiene practices, and launching a vaccination campaign. "When it comes to cholera, targeted prevention—including vaccination—is a priority. Of course, there is also a need to prepare for treatment of patients because the disease can very quickly be deadly. But this does not replace the importance of prevention, which aims to prevent the spread of the disease beyond the first cases,"[10] says Dr. Jean-Patrick Ouamba, deputy medical coordinator with Doctors Without Borders.

Public health officials also worked to educate patients, family members, and communities in at-risk areas about the disease and how it spreads. They provided education about hygiene practices such as washing hands before meals and after using the bathroom, treating water before use, washing vegetables and fruits before eating, and adequately cooking all foods.

Diseases Spread Through Water

Some infectious diseases, like cholera, are spread through water contaminated by microscopic organisms such as viruses and bacteria, chemicals, or other toxins. People can be infected with waterborne diseases when they drink contaminated water. Infection can also happen when a person breathes in contaminated water droplets or mist or when disease-carrying water enters the body through the ears or nose. A waterborne disease outbreak occurs when two or more people get the same illness after exposure to the same contaminated water source.

Common waterborne illnesses include cholera, cryptosporidiosis, cyclosporiasis, giardiasis, legionellosis, and other gastrointestinal diseases. Symptoms of waterborne illness most commonly include diarrhea and vomiting but may also include respiratory illnesses, skin problems, blood infections, and more.

wastewater

Any water that has been contaminated by human use

Outbreaks of waterborne diseases frequently occur after a severe rainfall or snowfall event. Heavy rains or snows can increase flooding and runoff, spreading microscopic organisms, sewage, and other disease agents that contaminate water sources. Heavy precipitation can also damage water sanitation facilities and expand breeding grounds for disease-causing microorganisms.

Improperly treated wastewater can be another source of waterborne disease. Wastewater is any water from ordinary living,

Wastewater Treatment

Wastewater treatment is an essential part of keeping water supplies safe. If wastewater is not treated to remove pathogens and pollutants, it can contaminate a community's water supplies. Adequate wastewater treatment involves several steps that remove or inactivate the contaminants and disease-causing microorganisms in the wastewater. First, solid materials are filtered out of the wastewater. Alternatively, solid materials or sludge can be removed after they settle and separate from the rest of the wastewater. Next, wastewater undergoes further filtration as well as biological and chemical processes. Liquids are stored for more time to allow for additional settling of sludge. Before disposal, sludge undergoes treatment with lime or chemicals, air drying, heat drying, or composting. The treated sludge can then be disposed of in several ways, including burning, use as commercial fertilizer, or burial in a landfill. Sometimes soil, sand, or similar material can filter and remove pollutants from liquid wastes. Finally, wastewater is disinfected. Chlorine, ozone, ultraviolet light, or other chemicals can inactivate many contaminants and pathogens in the wastewater before it is released from treatment facilities.

such as bathing, toilet flushing, laundry, and dishwashing. Homes, farms, hospitals, and businesses all generate wastewater. Some communities have sewer systems that collect wastewater and stormwater runoff. Untreated wastewater can contain disease-carrying feces and urine from humans and animals, as well as other contaminants. When untreated wastewater reaches drinking water sources, people may become sick.

Wastewater treatment improves and purifies water by removing some or all contaminants in the water. The purified water is then able to be reused or discharged back into the environment. When wastewater treatment is not sufficient, water can carry disease-causing organisms into homes and the environment.

Worldwide Waterborne Diseases

Every year, waterborne diseases affect hundreds of millions of people worldwide. Many of those sickened live in developing countries and do not have access to safe water. According to the WHO, 2.1 billion people worldwide lack access to safe, readily available water at home, while 4.5 billion lack adequate sanitation. "Safe water, effective sanitation and hygiene are critical to the health of every child and every community—and thus are essential to building stronger, healthier, and more equitable societies,"[11] says UNICEF executive director Anthony Lake.

Although not as common, waterborne diseases still sicken people in developed countries. According to the CDC, in the United States, which has one of the world's safest drinking water supplies, approximately 7.2 million people get sick annually from waterborne diseases. In 2017 several people who visited Disneyland in Anaheim, California, contracted Legionnaires' disease. Legionnaires' disease is a lung infection caused by exposure to water or mist contaminated with the *Legionella pneumophila* bacteria. Local health officials discovered twenty-two cases of waterborne illness among people who visited Disneyland or spent time in Anaheim. Several were hospitalized, and one died.

In 2017 several people who visited Disneyland in Anaheim, California, contracted Legionnaires' disease after being exposed to contaminated water or mist.

Investigating Waterborne Disease Outbreaks

Public health systems rely on surveillance and data collection to better understand how waterborne disease spreads and alert health officials when a potential outbreak occurs. Surveillance data, which tracks illness and disease, helps officials determine what efforts to use to reduce and prevent current and future outbreaks.

In the United States the national Waterborne Disease and Outbreak Surveillance System (WBDOSS) collects data from across the country on waterborne disease and outbreaks. The surveillance system gathers information on the number of outbreak-associated illnesses, hospitalizations, and deaths. It collects data on the type of water involved, water systems, and water locations. WBDOSS also tracks data on single cases of waterborne illness caused by certain chemicals or germs.

When a group of people becomes ill with similar symptoms simultaneously, local and state health departments investigate to determine what caused them to get sick. Outbreak investigations are critical because they help officials learn what pathogens cause illness, what types of water are involved, and the groups of people affected. With this information, officials can develop a plan to control a waterborne disease outbreak and prevent additional people from getting sick. They also learn how to prevent similar outbreaks in the future.

Determining the source of contaminated water can be complicated. Most people who get sick do not realize contaminated water caused their illness. Many germs spread by water can also be spread in other ways. For example, a person may get a stomach illness from eating contaminated food or being in close contact with another sick person. People drink and use water many times a day, which makes it difficult to pinpoint which specific exposure might be the one that caused the illness. Additionally, it can take days or weeks to become ill after being exposed to a waterborne pathogen, making it even harder to determine the source of the contaminated water.

Pools and Waterborne Disease

As summertime approaches, many families head to the local swimming pool for a day of fun. However, they might not want to jump in so fast. The CDC warns that swimming pools can be the source of many waterborne diseases. In particular, pools are often the source of cryptosporidiosis outbreaks every year. From 2009 to 2017, 444 cryptosporidiosis outbreaks were reported in the United States and Puerto Rico. More than a third of the cases were linked to recreation water sources, including swimming pools, kiddie pools, and water playgrounds. Cryptosporidiosis is an illness caused by the cryptosporidium parasite that causes watery diarrhea. It spreads by contact with the feces of an infected person or animal. In a swimming pool, an infected person can shed enough of the parasite to infect others. Because the parasite has a high tolerance to chlorine, it can survive for long periods in chlorinated swimming pools and other recreational water sources.

Investigating the Disneyland Outbreak

In an outbreak investigation, public health professionals work quickly to define and find cases. In 2017 the investigation into the Disneyland outbreak began when the CDC notified Orange County, California, health officials that several cases of Legionnaires' disease had occurred among people who had traveled to the county in September. Investigators interviewed the sick people and discovered that many of them had recently visited Disneyland or spent time in Anaheim near the theme park. Public health officials asked local medical professionals to test anyone who appeared to have similar symptoms for the infectious disease to discover additional cases. Eventually, investigators identified more than twenty cases.

Next, outbreak investigators develop a hypothesis about how these individuals became sick. In the Legionnaires' disease case, investigators suspected that water at Disneyland was the source of the outbreak. Nineteen of the twenty-two people had visited Disneyland in September or early October. Many Legionnaires' disease outbreaks are linked to cooling towers, which are part of an air-conditioning system and release mist. When cooling towers are not properly cleaned and disinfected, the moist environment creates an ideal place for *Legionella pneumophila* bacteria to grow.

Next, investigators take steps to control and contain the outbreak. In California investigators contacted theme park officials and alerted them to the outbreak. Disneyland personnel reported to health officials that testing of two water cooling towers had detected elevated levels of the *Legionella pneumophila* bacteria in October 2017. Disneyland park officials agreed to take the two cooling towers out of service on November 1. They disinfected the towers and performed more testing to confirm they were no longer contaminated with the *Legionella pneumophila* bacteria. "These towers were treated with chemicals that destroy the bacteria and are currently shut down,"[12] said Dr. Pamela Hymel, chief medical officer for Walt Disney Parks and Resorts.

epidemiology

The branch of medicine that studies how often diseases occur in human populations and why they occur

When no additional cases of Legionnaires' disease surfaced, public health officials determined that the outbreak was over. Dr. Matthew Zahn, medical director for epidemiology at the Orange County Health Care Agency, testified in 2018 before the California Occupational Safety and Health Administration that the Disneyland cooling towers were the likely outbreak source. Zahn explained that one of the Disneyland cooling towers tested positive for high levels of *Legionella pneumophila* bacteria at the same time people became sick. Once the tower was cleaned and disinfected, no additional cases of Legionnaires' disease emerged. "Most likely, those cases were related to a common exposure," Zahn said. "Cooling tower No. 4 was the most likely source of exposure."[13]

Disneyland officials denied that the park was the source of the outbreak and argued that three infected people had not visited the park. Zahn disagreed, explaining that contaminated droplets from the park's cooling towers could have spread in the air beyond the park. Additionally, when public health officials investigated other cooling towers in the area outside of the theme park, they found no significant evidence of *Legionella pneumophila* bacteria. "Though it would not be possible to definitely link the cases to (Disney's) cooling towers, the level of contamination and their location suggests that they are a potential source for some or all cases,"[14] said Jessica Good, spokesperson for the Orange County Health Care Agency's Environmental Health division.

Typhoid Fever in Zimbabwe

Since 2010 the CDC has worked with Zimbabwe's health officials to investigate suspected outbreaks of typhoid fever, a serious and life-threatening illness caused by the bacteria *Salmonella typhi*. In 2017 CDC health professionals assisted the Zimbabwe health ministry in investigating several suspected typhoid fever outbreaks. Many people rely on boreholes in Zimbabwe, deep wells drilled into the ground to reach underground water supplies.

Contaminated water from boreholes like this one caused hundreds of people in Zimbabwe to become ill with typhoid fever in 2017.

Typhoid fever can spread if sewage that contains the bacteria gets into the water used for drinking or washing food. The 2017 Zimbabwe investigation revealed that many of the boreholes near the outbreak were old, damaged, and contaminated with feces. Additionally, record rainfall had overwhelmed the region's sewer systems and caused them to overflow and contaminate the region's water sources. As a result, hundreds of people became ill.

The CDC team worked with local public health officials to respond to the outbreak quickly and effectively. Together, they helped laboratory staff acquire the technical skills needed to diagnose typhoid fever. They also implemented robust surveillance systems to gather and analyze data. The CDC team also supported local health officials in creating a national response plan for typhoid fever. In the community, public health officials and the CDC team promoted the importance of hygiene practices like washing hands before eating and after going to the bathroom and sanitation to prevent the spread of typhoid fever.

Access to safe, clean sources of water is an essential part of good health. When water becomes contaminated by microorganisms, chemicals, or other toxic materials, people can get sick. Every day, public health professionals worldwide work tirelessly to ensure communities detect, control, and prevent outbreaks small and large of waterborne infectious disease.

CHAPTER THREE

Diseases from Animals and Insects

Cases of dengue fever in Hawaii began to rise in September 2015. By the end of December, 180 cases of dengue fever had been confirmed on Hawaii's Big Island. Dengue fever is an infectious disease spread by mosquitoes and typically found in tropical and subtropical regions. Mild cases of dengue fever cause fever and flu-like symptoms. Severe cases, also called dengue hemorrhagic fever, can cause severe bleeding, a sudden drop in blood pressure, and death. Millions of cases of dengue fever occur every year around the world. Most cases occur in Southeast Asia, the western Pacific islands, Latin America, and Africa.

Although the United States does not typically have a high risk of dengue, local cases can occur when mosquitoes bite infected travelers and then bite others. "People come onto the island [Hawaii] infected with dengue and infect local mosquitos. That can set off a transmission cycle and start an outbreak,"[15] explains Dr. Lyle Petersen, a CDC expert on mosquito-borne infections.

In Hawaii health officials opened an investigation to identify additional dengue cases and potential sources of exposure. They sent a medical advisory to all health professionals in Hawaii and asked them to look out for and report any patients displaying possible dengue symptoms. From September 2015 to March 2016, health officials identified 264 confirmed cases of dengue.

Globally, the most effective public health methods used to fight the spread of mosquito-borne viral infections like dengue prevent mosquito bites and control an area's mosquito population. Therefore, with each reported possible dengue case, Hawaii's health officials surveyed areas around the patient's home and work for heavy mosquito activity. They searched these areas for potential mosquito breeding grounds, such as puddles or other standing water sources. Officials treated and sprayed the sites in an attempt to limit mosquito activity. Even with these prevention efforts, Petersen acknowledges that curbing mosquito-borne illness is a challenge. "These mosquitoes are very, very difficult to control," he says. "In any urban environment, mosquitoes are common and breed in many, many locations. It's difficult if not impossible to get rid of all the breeding sites."[16]

In tropical and subtropical regions such as Southeast Asia, the Pacific islands, Latin America, and Africa, mosquitoes like this one spread dengue fever, which in mild cases leads to flu-like symptoms, but in severe cases can lead to death.

In addition to spraying to reduce mosquito populations, health department officials rolled out the Fight the Bite public education campaign. They urged Hawaii residents and tourists to wear protective clothing with long sleeves and long pants and use mosquito repellents to prevent bites. They also encouraged residents to eliminate potential breeding sites on their property.

By April 2016 the Hawaii health department reported no additional cases of dengue fever. Through public health measures, the state could contain the outbreak and limit the number of people infected. The health department plans to continue routine monitoring for future imported dengue fever cases along with pesticide spraying and outbreak containment as needed.

Insects and Disease

Some infectious diseases like dengue fever spread to people from insects (vectors) and are called vector-borne diseases. Bloodsucking insects such as mosquitoes, ticks, and fleas can all transmit disease. When these insects bite an infected human or animal, they can acquire disease-causing microorganisms such as viruses, bacteria, and parasites from the infected person's blood. As the pathogen reproduces in the insect, the insect becomes infectious. When the infectious insect bites a healthy person, it passes the pathogen to the healthy person, which causes a new infection. Often, an infectious insect can transmit the disease-producing pathogen in every bite for the rest of its life span.

vector-borne disease

Infectious diseases spread by insects such as mosquitoes, ticks, and fleas

Vector-borne diseases are often difficult to prevent and control. Few have effective vaccines to protect people from them. According to the WHO, every year, vector-borne diseases make up more than 17 percent of all infectious diseases. They cause more than seven hundred thousand deaths per year. Some vector-borne diseases like the plague have existed for centuries. Others have only

Antimicrobial Resistance

For years, antimicrobial medicines—antibiotics, antivirals, antifungals, and anti-parasitics—have been used to prevent and treat many infections in humans and animals. In recent years, however, the overuse of these medications has led to antimicrobial resistance. Antimicrobial resistance occurs when the bacteria, viruses, fungi, and parasites mutate and are no longer effectively treated by existing medications. This drug resistance makes infectious diseases harder to treat and increases the risk of diseases spreading and making others ill. For zoonotic diseases, the use of antibiotics in animals raised for food has increased the risk of zoonotic pathogens becoming drug resistant and more likely to spread in both animals and humans.

been recently discovered. Today some common vector-borne diseases include malaria, dengue, yellow fever, Lyme disease, West Nile virus, Zika, and more.

Vector-borne diseases commonly occur in tropical and subtropical regions, where conditions are ideal for disease-carrying insects to breed and thrive. However, increasing global travel and urbanization have led to vector-borne disease outbreaks in new areas. Even though the United States is not generally a hot spot for vector-borne disease, cases have become more common in recent years. According to the CDC, vector-borne disease cases in the United States more than doubled from 2004 to 2018.

In the United States, Lyme disease is the most common vector-borne illness. Every year an estimated three hundred thousand infections occur. Lyme disease is caused by an infection by the *Borrelia burgdorferi* bacteria. Transmitted to humans by the bite of an infected black-legged tick, Lyme disease causes symptoms of fever, headache, fatigue, and rash. West Nile virus is another vector-borne disease that has become increasingly common in the United States. Every summer, outbreaks of the virus occur. Most people infected with West Nile virus have no symptoms, but some develop a severe and sometimes fatal illness.

Disease Spread by Animals

Every day people interact with animals at home, at work, in outdoor spaces, and in other places. Animals provide food, travel, sport, and companionship for many people. However, animals can also carry harmful pathogens that can spread to people and cause illness. Zoonotic diseases are infectious diseases that have spread from animals to humans.

Zoonotic diseases are caused by harmful viruses, bacteria, parasites, and fungi. These pathogens cause many different illnesses in both humans and animals. Some zoonotic diseases cause only a mild illness, while others can be deadly. Zoonotic diseases around the world are common. According to the WHO, there are over two hundred known zoonotic diseases. They make up a large percentage of both new and existing diseases in humans. According to the CDC, as many as six out of ten known infectious diseases in humans can be spread from animals. Also, three out of every four emerging infectious diseases in humans come from animals. Some zoonotic diseases, such as human immunodeficiency virus (HIV), an infectious disease that attacks the body's immune system, later mutate into into a human-only strain.

zoonotic disease

Infectious diseases spread from animals to humans

Zoonotic diseases can spread from animals to people at any point of contact. A person can become sick by coming into direct contact with an infected animal's body fluids, such as saliva, blood, urine, mucus, or feces. Infection can also spread when a person pets or touches an infected animal or gets bitten or scratched.

Zoonotic diseases can also spread through indirect contact with infected animals. Indirect contact includes exposure to areas where the infected animal lives or objects that the infected animal has touched and that now carry the pathogen, such as aquariums, chicken coops, or food and water dishes. Some zoonotic diseases can spread to humans from eating food or drinking water that has been contaminated by feces from an infected animal.

Rabies is an example of a zoonotic disease. The rabies virus affects the central nervous system. Without treatment, rabies can affect the brain and eventually cause death. Around the world, dogs are the most common animals that carry rabies. In the United States rabies is more often found in wild animals such as raccoons, skunks, bats, and foxes. The rabies virus can spread from animal to human when a person is bitten or scratched by an infected animal.

In Haiti rabies is a significant problem. Street dogs frequently carry the virus and transmit it to humans. Every week an average of two people in Haiti die from rabies. Most of the time, those who died of a rabies infection did not receive adequate treatment after being bitten by a disease-carrying dog. To control the spread of rabies and prevent rabies deaths, the CDC's National Center for Emerging and Zoonotic Infectious Diseases (NCEZID) is working with Haiti's health officials to implement and strengthen public health measures. They have implemented a program to vacci-

Wild animals such as raccoons can carry rabies, which can be spread to humans if they are bitten or scratched by an infected animal.

nate local dogs to prevent them from developing rabies. Health officials have also improved surveillance systems to allow them to detect and identify rabies cases more quickly. For those who have been bitten by dogs, health professionals focus on providing the necessary treatment to prevent a severe rabies infection. As a result of these efforts, more than 110,000 dogs have been vaccinated, and almost one hundred animal health professionals are monitoring Haiti's animal populations for rabies cases. These public health measures have enabled officials to increase rabies detection eighteen-fold. Also, better treatment of people who have been bitten is in place. Post-bite vaccination of people at risk of developing rabies has increased by 230 percent. As a result, fewer people are becoming seriously ill, and the risk of dying from rabies has decreased by 49 percent in Haiti.

Detect and Prevent

Public health departments worldwide work to detect and prevent the spread of infectious diseases transmitted by insects and animals. In the United States the CDC's NCEZID and Division of Vector-Borne Diseases focus specifically on these types of infectious diseases. Both centers work with local health departments to quickly detect and monitor threats from vector-borne and zoonotic diseases. To do this, they employ tools such as ArboNET, a national surveillance system that tracks vector-borne viruses in humans, animals, and mosquitoes. Other surveillance systems collect data on other vector-borne and zoonotic diseases.

Once possible cases of illness are identified, health officials rely on cutting-edge laboratory testing to quickly identify and diagnose new cases of vector-borne and zoonotic diseases. Investigators also conduct interviews with sick people to determine who they have been in contact with and find additional disease cases that have not yet been reported to public health officials.

In 2016 the Oak Leaf Dairy Farm in Connecticut held several events in which the public could visit the farm and pet its goats.

After one of these events, several people fell ill in an outbreak of *Escherichia coli* (E. coli) infections. E. coli is a bacterium that is found in animal and human feces and can also be found in contaminated food. Symptoms of an E. coli infection include diarrhea, vomiting, cramping, and fever. When local health officials interviewed the sick people, they discovered that several had recently visited the goat farm. Public health officials immediately notified the farm's owner of the farm's potential connection to the E. coli outbreak. To prevent further disease spread, the farm's owner closed the farm to the public during the investigation.

As part of the outbreak investigation, officials visited the farm and collected environmental samples from the farm's animals and surfaces. Laboratory testing confirmed the outbreak strain of E. coli in twenty-eight out of sixty-one environmental samples. Also, sixteen of seventeen fecal samples from the goats contained the outbreak strain of E. coli bacteria. Investigators also observed that farm visitors were given direct access to the animals and soiled bedding. They noted no handwashing stations on the farm and no signs prompting visitors to wash their hands after touching the animals. In total, fifty confirmed cases of E. coli infection were linked to the outbreak. Of those cases, forty people had visited the farm, while six others had contact with someone who had visited the farm. Because E. coli can spread quickly, particularly among family members, Connecticut public health officials reminded residents to wash their hands consistently. "The best way to prevent the spread of infection is to wash your hands thoroughly after contact with animals and after going to the bathroom and by thoroughly cooking meats and washing fruits and vegetables,"[17] stated the Connecticut Department of Public Health.

Several public health measures are effective in reducing the risk of zoonotic disease in a community. Safe animal care guidelines and educational programs that emphasize handwashing and hygiene practices can reduce the spread of zoonotic disease. After the E. coli outbreak, Connecticut public health offi-

Detecting Outbreaks with Gene Sequencing Technology

In recent years new technologies have allowed public health laboratories to decode the DNA of infectious disease pathogens better. Using the latest gene sequencing machines, scientists can decode a pathogen's whole genome in high resolution. The high-tech sequencing machines enable scientists to sequence a pathogen's DNA faster than ever, up to 8 billion DNA base pairs per day. Sequencing can even occur outside of the lab. High-tech handheld units allow sequencing to happen in the field, helping public health officials with infectious disease surveillance, diagnosis, and research.

With whole-genome sequencing, scientists can create a detailed DNA fingerprint of a disease-causing pathogen. In public health, epidemiologists and laboratory scientists can use this detailed fingerprint to identify and link cases in an outbreak more quickly. A DNA fingerprint also helps public health officials detect an outbreak that may not have been previously detected.

cials and partners created a program for farmers to learn about animal safety and sanitation. They hope the education program will prevent similar outbreaks in the future. They also developed educational videos for families about the importance of supervising young children around animals and the importance of handwashing to prevent infectious disease spread.

Tracking Bats in Uganda

In Uganda, African fruit bats have been identified as the source of several devastating outbreaks of Marburg hemorrhagic fever, a rare but severe illness in humans and primates. Marburg hemorrhagic fever is caused by the Marburg virus, a virus closely related to Ebola. The disease-carrying fruit bat typically lives in caves across Africa and has been linked to outbreaks in several countries. Many of the outbreaks began with mine workers who worked in bat-infested mines. Once infected by the bats, the mine workers spread the virus through their communities.

To help prevent future outbreaks of the virus, the CDC has worked with Ugandan officials to place Global Positioning System

African fruit bats have been identified as the source of several outbreaks of Marburg hemorrhagic fever, a severe illness in humans and primates.

(GPS) units in the bats' backs. The GPS units will track the bats' movements so that health officials can learn where they travel. With this information, public health officials hope to be able to more accurately predict which regions have the highest risk of Marburg virus infection and be better able to prevent the next outbreak.

Animals, insects, and humans coexist in every place on earth. In some cases, infectious diseases carried by animals and insects can spread to humans, sometimes with devastating consequences. Public health systems worldwide work with communities to detect, prevent, and control infectious disease outbreaks spread by animals and insects. Because of their work, many people are living healthier lives.

CHAPTER FOUR

Person-to-Person Infectious Diseases

In 2009 a novel influenza A (H1N1) virus appeared. The new flu virus was first detected in the United States. It spread quickly across the country and around the world. The new H1N1 virus was very different from other known H1N1 viruses. This one was made of a unique combination of influenza genes that had not been previously identified in people or animals. Because the new H1N1 virus was so different from other H1N1 viruses circulating at the time, existing flu vaccination provided little protection against the new strain. By June 2009 the WHO declared a pandemic, an outbreak of infectious disease worldwide. It was the first global flu pandemic in forty years.

From April 2009 to April 2010, the CDC estimated 60.8 million cases of H1N1 infection in the United States. Of those, about 274,000 people were sick enough to be hospitalized, while more than 12,000 died. Worldwide, the CDC estimated 151,000 to 575,000 people died from the new H1N1 virus in the first year it appeared.

In response to the H1N1 pandemic, US public health officials worked to learn more about the new infectious disease, how it spread, and how to control it. The CDC teamed up with state and local health officials on epidemiological investigations. They interviewed sick patients and traced their contacts to identify the infection sources. They used surveillance systems to detect additional cases of H1N1. Based on the information learned in their investigations, CDC scientists believed that the virus had been transmitted from person to person. In the community, public health officials urged people to prevent the virus's spread by staying home if they felt sick and covering their mouth and nose when coughing or sneezing.

Fighting H1N1

CDC scientists also worked to identify complete gene sequences of the 2009 H1N1 virus. They uploaded their work into an international influenza database, which gave scientists worldwide the ability to use gene sequencing for research and to compare the H1N1 virus against influenza viruses detected in other parts of the world. CDC scientists also developed a new diagnostic test to help health care professionals quickly and accurately diagnose cases of H1N1 in patients.

In 2009 people lined up in Omaha, Nebraska, to receive a vaccination against the H1N1 influenza virus.

At the same time, scientists developed a vaccine to protect against the new flu virus. In September 2009 the FDA announced its approval of four new vaccines to protect against the 2009 H1N1 influenza virus. The FDA approved the fifth vaccine in November. With these vaccines, public health officials launched a national vaccination campaign beginning in October 2009.

asymptomatic carrier

An infected person who shows no symptoms of disease but can still transmit it

Eventually, the efforts of public health officials worldwide brought the virus under control. In August 2010 the WHO declared that the global 2009 H1N1 influenza pandemic had ended. Despite the public health success, the H1N1 virus was not entirely eliminated. It continues to surface as a seasonal flu virus, causing illness, hospitalization, and deaths every year.

Like the H1N1 virus, many infectious diseases are primarily transmitted from person to person. These diseases include acute respiratory infections, sexually transmitted diseases, measles, mumps, and streptococcal infections. Sometimes, a person carrying an infectious disease may not show any signs of illness. These asymptomatic carriers can still infect others with the disease. Other times, infection spreads during an incubation period, when an infected person can transmit an infection before becoming sick. Other times, an infected person may have recovered from an illness but can still pass on the pathogen to others.

incubation period

The time between exposure to a pathogen and when a person experiences signs or symptoms of infection

Acute Respiratory Infections

Acute respiratory infections are some of the world's most deadly infectious diseases. According to the WHO, lower respiratory infections were the world's most deadly infectious diseases in 2019

Overwhelmed by Outbreaks

Outbreaks of infectious diseases can overwhelm health systems and cause severe illness and death. Because many hospitals operate near their capacity during regular times, there is not much spare room for increased numbers of patients during an outbreak. When an outbreak occurs, health care systems must balance limited resources—doctors, nurses, hospital rooms, medicines, equipment, and medical supplies—with greater patient needs. Sometimes, this means that patients cannot get the treatment they need.

In January 2021 a surge in the COVID-19 pandemic stretched health systems in Southern California almost to the breaking point. Hospitals admitted thousands of sick people. Public health projections forecast that thousands more would need hospital care in the coming weeks. Facing shortages of staff and supplies, many hospitals prepared to ration care. According to guidelines released by the Los Angeles County Department of Public Health, "Decisions of allocation will be to decide which patients get which resource, and in some circumstances, may involve decisions to take scarce resources from one patient and give them to another who is more likely to benefit from them."

Quoted in Stella Chan and Cheri Mossburg, "L.A. County Hospitals Prepare for Triage Officers to Ration Care as Covid-19 Cases Overwhelm," CNN.com, January 8, 2021. www.cnn.com.

and caused 2.6 million deaths. Respiratory infections ranked as the fourth leading cause of death in 2019, behind heart disease, stroke, and chronic obstructive pulmonary disease. Examples of acute respiratory diseases include pneumonia, influenza, tuberculosis, severe acute respiratory syndrome, Middle East respiratory syndrome (MERS), respiratory syncytial virus, and H1N1 influenza. The 2019 novel coronavirus that causes COVID-19 is another example of respiratory infectious disease.

Many pathogens that cause acute respiratory infections spread when a person coughs or sneezes and releases respiratory droplets into the air or onto surfaces. Healthy people become infected if they inhale disease-carrying respiratory droplets. They can also become infected by touching an object or surface exposed to the germs and then touching their nose or mouth, which allows the pathogen to enter the body.

Infectious respiratory diseases can spread far and wide in a very short amount of time. Today, an infected person can fly around the world in a matter of hours or days. Along the way, they can spread infected respiratory droplets to people in close contact with them, who go on to spread the disease further. "In our interconnected world, pathogens can travel rapidly, and outbreaks can occur in unexpected places," says Dr. Shin Young-soo, WHO regional director for the Western Pacific. "All countries . . . must remain alert for the possibility of an imported case of . . . [an] infectious disease and be ready to respond swiftly and efficiently."[18]

In 2015 a traveler from the Middle East infected with Middle East respiratory syndrome (MERS) coronavirus entered Korea. First reported in Saudi Arabia in 2012, MERS is a viral respiratory disease that causes a severe illness with fever, cough, and shortness of breath. Many people infected with MERS have died. By June 2015 Korean health officials confirmed thirty cases of the MERS virus, all of which were linked to the Middle East traveler. Korean public health officials and WHO officials worked quickly to contain the outbreak of the MERS virus. Public health officials identified and isolated all confirmed and suspected cases of the virus. They conducted contact tracing to identify and quarantine all contacts of the ill patients. They also improved infection prevention and control procedures in local hospitals and health care settings to prevent the further spread of the virus. By the end of the outbreak in July 2015, laboratory testing confirmed 186 cases of the virus. Additionally, thirty-eight people died from the virus.

Investigating Respiratory Disease Outbreaks

While acute respiratory diseases are common, investigating an outbreak can be challenging. One of the most challenging tasks for public health officials is to identify the pathogen causing an outbreak. Many pathogens behind respiratory disease cause similar symptoms, making it difficult to determine an illness's exact cause. Additionally, diagnostic tests may not be locally available to help health care professionals quickly and accurately diagnose new cases of the disease. However, identifying the specific pathogen behind the illness is critical to treating sick patients and containing an outbreak.

When a respiratory disease outbreak occurs, public health investigators gather information through interviews with patients, contacts, and health professionals. They collect specimens from infected patients. These specimens get sent to laboratories, where they are tested to identify the pathogen or pathogens involved. Investigators use surveillance systems to determine the number of cases and severity of illness experienced by infected patients.

Public Health Response

With the information gathered about the illness and outbreak, public health officials develop a response to control the outbreak and prevent further infection. In the case of acute respiratory diseases, a public health response may include measures such as quarantine and isolation, contact tracing, mask wearing, and vaccination.

When the 2019 coronavirus spread around the globe in 2020 and 2021, public health officials worldwide implemented various measures to slow the spread of the highly contagious virus. Many countries closed their borders, schools, and businesses. They instituted lockdowns and ordered citizens to stay at home—for weeks or months at a time. When communities began to reopen, many governments required citizens to wear masks and practice social distancing, restricted the operation of schools and some businesses, and limited the size of public and private gatherings.

Sexually Transmitted Infectious Diseases

In some cases, infectious diseases spread through sexual contact. Sexually transmitted diseases (STDs) are common in the United States, with millions of new infections occurring annually. According to the CDC, one in five people in the United States had a sexually transmitted infection in 2018. If untreated, STDs can

A pregnant woman who is infected with syphilis, a sexually transmitted disease (STD), can transmit the disease to her baby, leading to miscarriage, stillbirth, and newborn death.

spread to others and cause serious health effects such as infertility and ectopic pregnancy. Untreated STDs can also increase the risk of HIV, a virus that attacks the body's immune system. According to the WHO, "There is a strong link between sexually transmitted diseases (STDs) and the sexual transmission of HIV infection. The presence of an untreated STD can enhance both the acquisition and transmission of HIV by a factor of up to 10. Thus STD treatment is an important HIV prevention strategy in a general population."[19]

Another serious complication can occur in pregnant women who have an STD called syphilis. Infected mothers can pass the disease to their babies

ectopic

In an abnormal place, such as in pregnancy when a fetus develops outside the uterus

Controlling a Meningitis Outbreak

Across Africa bacterial meningitis has been endemic for decades, which means it regularly occurs in the population, with outbreaks striking from time to time. Bacterial meningitis is a severe infection caused by several types of bacteria. Even when treated with antibiotics, 10 to 15 percent of patients will die. Those who survive often have hearing loss, brain damage, or paralysis. While bacterial meningitis spreads through person-to-person contact, how the bacteria spreads depends on the type of bacteria involved. Therefore, identifying the specific bacteria involved in an outbreak is essential.

From December 2015 to February 2016, Ghana public officials tracked an outbreak of bacterial meningitis. They partnered with CDC experts to perform real-time polymerase chain reaction testing to detect and identify the disease-causing bacteria in the patient's specimens. This laboratory analysis enabled officials to quickly and accurately identify the infectious bacteria involved in the meningitis outbreak. The testing showed that most of the meningitis cases were caused by a type of bacteria that a vaccine could prevent. With this information, Ghana's health ministry launched a vaccine campaign that inoculated more than 98 percent of the people living in high-risk regions and prevented the additional spread of meningitis.

during pregnancy, leading to miscarriage, stillbirth, and newborn death. Babies who survive may suffer from severe physical and neurological problems. "STDs can come at a high cost for babies and other vulnerable populations," says Jonathan Mermin, director of the CDC's National Center for HIV/AIDS, Viral Hepatitis, STD, and TB Prevention. "Curbing STDs will improve the overall health of the nation and prevent infertility, HIV, and infant deaths."[20]

According to the CDC, STD rates in the United States have been rising in recent years. To slow the rise in STD infections, public health workers have promoted STD testing in affected communities. After a January 2019 spike in local syphilis cases in Philadelphia, public health workers offered free weekly syphilis testing at drop-in centers where homeless women at high risk for the STD visited for food and clothing. According to Cherie Walker-Baban, a program manager in the Philadelphia Department of Public

Health's STD Control Program, a rise in syphilis cases often occurs when there is an addiction crisis such as the opioid epidemic. "It's never-ending," says Walker-Baban. "We may not see a disease for a while, but when it shows its head, we have to go full force at it so it doesn't get out of control."[21]

For many local public health departments, outreach and education are key measures used to control the spread of STDs. These units work to increase awareness in their communities about the risk and impact of STDs. Many units offer confidential counseling, screening, testing, and treatment for a variety of STDs. They also provide school- and community-based education and awareness programs about STDs and their impact. To provide better care for those infected, local health officials consult with health care workers about the diagnosis and treatment of STDs. Some even offer free condoms to prevent the spread of infection.

Because of the stigma surrounding STDs, many people who might have an STD are embarrassed to get tested or warn sexual partners if they are positive. Without testing and notification, STD infections go untreated and can spread through a community. To address this barrier, the Connecticut Department of Public Health launched a video campaign in 2019 called #LeaveItToUs to reduce the spread of STDs in the state. The video campaign attempts to convince people to get tested by promoting the department's confidential testing and notification system. Says STD Control Program coordinator Dr. Lynn Sosa:

> We understand that having an STD can be scary. The message of the #LeaveItToUs campaign is simple: our staff is here to help make sure people are treated and assist in the process of telling their partners they should be tested too. Though it can be embarrassing to talk about, sharing information between sexual partners is critical to getting tested and treated, and ultimately reducing the spread of these diseases.[22]

When a person tests positive for an STD, trained staff with the STD Control Program talk to the person confidentially about his or her test results, treatment options, and potential partners who may have been exposed. Staff then reach out privately to the exposed partners without revealing the positive person's identity, inform them of their STD exposure, and encourage them to seek testing and treatment.

Infectious diseases spread from person to person can be some of the most common and most deadly diseases in the world. Public health officials work tirelessly to understand these diseases, how they spread, and the most effective measures for containing them.

CHAPTER FIVE

Saving Lives with Vaccines

On November 9, 2020, American biotechnology company Pfizer and its partner BioNTech, a German biotechnology company, announced that they had successfully developed an effective vaccine to protect against COVID-19, the illness caused by the 2019 coronavirus infectious disease. In clinical trials, Pfizer's vaccine was more than 90 percent effective in preventing COVID-19. The announcement signaled a significant step toward fighting the 2019 coronavirus pandemic, which had infected more than 116 million people and killed nearly 2.6 million people worldwide through early March 2021.

To slow the spread of the novel coronavirus that caused COVID-19, people worldwide had taken many public health measures to limit exposure and infection, such as isolation, quarantine, mask wearing, and social distancing. However, the development of a vaccine was a necessary breakthrough to protect health worldwide. Dr. Albert Bourla, Pfizer chair and chief executive officer (CEO), said at a November 2020 press conference:

Today is a great day for science and humanity. The first set of results from our Phase 3 COVID-19 vaccine trial provides the initial evidence of our vaccine's ability to prevent COVID-19. We are reaching this critical milestone in our vaccine development program at a time when the world needs it most with infection rates setting new records, hospitals nearing over-capacity and economies struggling to reopen. With today's news, we are a significant step closer to providing people around the world with a much-needed breakthrough to help bring an end to this global health crisis.[23]

On December 11, 2020, the FDA issued an emergency use authorization to allow the Pfizer-BioNTech COVID-19 vaccine to be used in the United States. "Today's emergency use authorization of the Pfizer-BioNTech COVID-19 Vaccine holds the promise to alter the course of this pandemic in the United States,"[24] said Dr. Peter Marks, director of the FDA's Center for Biologics Evaluation and Research. Within days, the first Americans received the vaccine shot. Sandra Lindsay, a critical-care nurse at Long Island

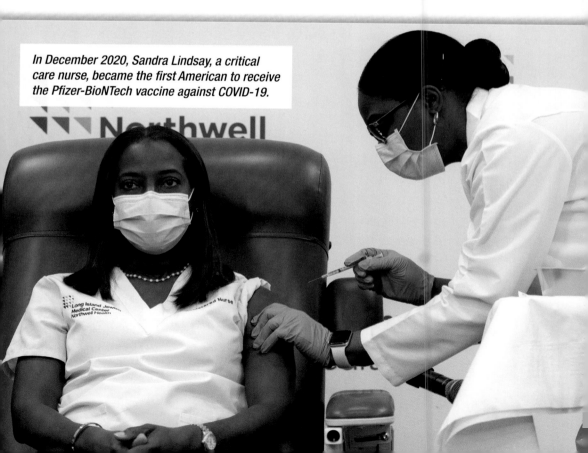

In December 2020, Sandra Lindsay, a critical care nurse, became the first American to receive the Pfizer-BioNTech vaccine against COVID-19.

Jewish Medical Center in Queens, received the first vaccine dose in the United States. She urges others to get vaccinated when it is their turn. "It is rooted in science, I trust science, and the alternative and what I have seen and experienced is far worse," she says. "So it's important that everyone pulls together to take the vaccine, not only to protect themselves but also to protect everyone they will come into contact with."[25]

Vaccines like the COVID-19 vaccine have played an essential role in protecting public health. Every year, vaccines save millions of lives. They work with the body's natural defenses to protect against germs and disease. According to the WHO, scientists have created vaccines that prevent more than twenty life-threatening diseases, such as tetanus, measles, polio, and influenza. "The facts are that vaccines work and America's pharmacists support vaccination as an important public health measure," says Thomas E. Menighan, American Pharmacists Association executive vice president and CEO. "Vaccines were created to protect the public against harmful and potentially deadly diseases. Because of vaccinations, many dangerous diseases are now preventable."[26]

How the Body Fights Infection

The body's immune system protects a person against infectious pathogens. Most pathogens are tiny microbes, such as bacteria, viruses, fungi, and parasites. All of these microbes can cause infections in the body. Through a series of steps called the immune response, the immune system attacks invaders in the body that cause disease.

White blood cells are one of the main components of the immune system. These cells seek out and destroy disease-causing germs. They move through the body using lymphatic vessels and blood vessels. Lymphocytes are a type of white blood cell that remembers, recognizes, and helps destroy

antigen

A foreign substance that produces an immune response in the body

mRNA Vaccines

Messenger RNA (mRNA) vaccines are a new type of vaccine used to protect people against infectious diseases. In human cells, mRNA is the genetic material that carries instructions for making proteins. Scientists have developed ways to use mRNA to teach cells how to make a protein that will trigger an immune response in the body. The immune response causes the body to think it is being attacked and produce antibodies to fight the attacker. When a real pathogen enters the body, the immune system is prepared to defend against it. Some of the new COVID-19 vaccines are examples of mRNA vaccines. These vaccines use mRNA to deliver instructions to the body's cells to make a piece of the spike protein found on the surface of the coronavirus that causes the COVID-19 illness. Each cell displays the spike protein on its surface. When a person's immune system recognizes that the spike protein is an invader, it triggers an immune response and starts making antibodies. This process mimics what the body would do in a natural COVID-19 infection. As a result, the immune system learns how to make the antibodies needed to defeat a future COVID-19 infection without the person ever becoming sick.

the germs. There are two types of lymphocytes: B lymphocytes and T lymphocytes. B lymphocytes function like military intelligence. They travel around the body and seek out targets. When they find a disease-causing antigen, they send signals to the T lymphocytes. The T lymphocytes are the immune system's first-line soldiers. They rush in and attack the antigens.

The body recognizes invaders that have tried to attack it before and remembers how to defeat them. When pathogens invade the body and are detected by the immune system, B lymphocytes produce specialized proteins that lock onto and tag specific antigens. These proteins are called antibodies. Antibodies are markers that signal T lymphocytes to attack the antigen.

Once produced, antibodies stay in the body. If the immune system detects a specific antigen again, the antibodies are already there to identify it for an attack.

antibodies

Markers produced by white blood cells that identify foreign substances in the body and help trigger the body's immune response

The first time a germ enters the body, it can take several days for the immune system to respond. However, after that first infection, the body's immune system remembers the germ and how to protect the body from it. If the germ returns, the body can quickly ramp up to fight the infection and protect the body.

How Vaccines Work to Protect Health

Vaccines work by kicking the body's immune system into action. A vaccine imitates an infection and tricks the body into thinking that it needs to gear up to fight the intruder. To protect the body, the immune system begins producing infection-fighting cells. Sometimes, a person may experience slight chills, low fever, or body aches after receiving a vaccination. When these symptoms occur, they usually disappear within a day or so. The person is not sick; instead, the symptoms are caused by the body's immune system working hard to create the antibodies needed to protect against the imitation pathogen. Once the body has produced antibodies for the first time in response to the vaccine, the immune system

Someone who receives a vaccination may experience mild symptoms such as chills, a low fever, and body aches as part of the immune response.

knows how to fight the pathogen. If the real pathogen enters the body in the future, the body's immune system can quickly produce the right antibodies to fight the pathogen and prevent illness.

There are several types of vaccines. Each works in a slightly different way. Some vaccines use small amounts of live, weakened viruses to produce an immune response. Vaccines for measles, mumps, and chicken pox are made this way. Other vaccines use viruses that have been inactivated or killed by a chemical, such as polio, rabies, and influenza vaccines. Some vaccines create an immune response by using part of the virus or bacteria. And while some vaccines are fully effective after one dose, others require multiple doses or even an annual dose to deliver the best protection. Despite the variation in how vaccines work, they all accomplish the same goal: to activate the body's immune system to fight and protect against infection.

Vaccine Success

Safe and effective vaccines have saved lives worldwide. From 1980 to 2020, the percentage of children worldwide who had received lifesaving vaccines jumped from about 20 percent to 86 percent. These vaccines protect the children and the communities where they live against several infectious diseases, including polio, measles, whooping cough, hepatitis B, diphtheria, and tetanus.

The polio vaccine is one example of how vaccines can significantly improve health. In the first half of the 1900s, polio was one of the most feared infectious diseases in the United States. Polio is a highly contagious infectious disease that travels through the bloodstream and can infect the brain and spinal cord. When the virus attacks the nervous system, paralysis can occur. Polio spreads when the feces of an infected person contaminates the water or food supply. Because the virus is so contagious, direct contact with a person infected with polio can also spread the disease.

In the late 1940s, polio outbreaks increased in frequency and size in the United States. These outbreaks paralyzed more than

The Development of a Vaccine

Vaccines are carefully developed through a rigorous testing process to make sure they are safe and effective. Scientists first test an experimental vaccine on animals to ensure it is safe and prevents disease. Then they test the vaccine in a series of human clinical trials. In Phase 1 trials, a small number of human volunteers receive the vaccine. Scientists make sure it is safe and generates an immune response; then they determine the proper dose. In Phase 2 trials, hundreds of volunteers receive the vaccine, while others do not. Scientists closely monitor the vaccine group for side effects and immune response. They also compare outcomes for the two groups. In Phase 3 trials, thousands of volunteers are split into two groups: some receive the vaccine, while a control group does not. Scientists compare the data and outcomes for the two groups to ensure the vaccine is safe and effective at protecting against disease.

Once clinical trials have demonstrated that the vaccine is safe and effective, regulatory and public health agencies review it before it is approved for use. Even after a vaccine is in use, scientists continue to monitor it for unexpected side effects and effectiveness.

thirty-five thousand people annually. When the virus peaked during the summer months, parents were afraid to let their children go outside. Cities experiencing polio outbreaks restricted travel. Public health officials quarantined people who had possibly been exposed to the disease.

In 1955 and 1963 scientists introduced polio vaccines. As Americans became vaccinated, the spread of the disease quickly slowed. There were fewer than one hundred polio cases across the country in the 1960s. By the 1970s there were fewer than ten polio cases in the United States. Because of the polio vaccine's success, the United States has not recorded a case of polio since 1979, according to the CDC.

Using Vaccines to Fight Ebola

From 2014 to 2016, an outbreak of Ebola virus disease struck West Africa. Ebola is a rare but deadly disease in humans and primates. Ebola spreads through direct contact with an infected

Workers in Liberia bury the body of an Ebola victim. Because Ebola can be spread by contact with a person who died of the disease, health care workers must wear special garments to protect them from infection.

animal, the body fluids of an infected person, or a person who has died from the disease. In the West African epidemic, more than eleven thousand people died from Ebola, according to the WHO.

To protect against future deadly outbreaks of Ebola, scientists quickly worked on a vaccine. The WHO funded vaccine research, fast-tracked clinical trials of potential vaccine candidates, and sped required regulatory approvals. Working night and day, scientists moved from early testing to vaccine trials in only ten months. Trials in Guinea found the vaccine to be highly effective against Ebola.

When the Democratic Republic of the Congo (DRC) detected a new Ebola virus outbreak in May 2018, the vaccine was recommended for use. Public health officials gave the vaccine to contacts of confirmed cases, contacts of contacts, health care workers, first responders, and others with potential exposure to the deadly virus. "Vaccination is a new and vital tool in the control of Ebola," said Dr. Michael Ryan, WHO assistant director general of emergency preparedness and response. "I just spent the day out with the vaccination teams in the community, and for the first time in my experience, I saw hope in the face of Ebola and not terror. This is a major milestone for global public health."[27]

For Jean René, who lost his brother to Ebola virus disease, getting vaccinated has given him peace of mind for himself and the rest of his family. René lives near Mbandaka, one of the first areas in the DRC to report confirmed Ebola cases during the May outbreak. Because René and his extended family were considered high-risk contacts of a person with Ebola, public health officials vaccinated the entire family.

In August 2018 Ebola struck the eastern regions of the DRC. Public health officials quickly launched a vaccination campaign to limit the spread of the disease. From August 2018 to March 2020, more than three hundred thousand people received Ebola vaccinations. The public health efforts and vaccinations slowed the spread of Ebola. In June 2020 the WHO declared the nearly two-year-long DRC Ebola outbreak over. In total, the WHO reported about 3,500 cases of Ebola. Of these, 2,299 people died from the disease.

Throughout the world, public health professionals work hard to detect, contain, and prevent infectious disease outbreaks. As they learn more about new and emerging disease-causing pathogens, public health systems are better able to design and implement measures to protect communities from disease.

Introduction: Preventing Outbreaks Worldwide

1. Quoted in Michelle Roberts, "Zika-Linked Condition: WHO Declares Global Emergency," *BBC*, February 1, 2016. www.bbc.com.
2. Quoted in Pam Belluck and Donald G. McNeil Jr., "Zika Virus Causes Birth Defects, Health Officials Confirm," *New York Times*, April 13, 2016. www.nytimes.com.
3. Quoted in Roberts, "Zika-Linked Condition."

Chapter One: Foodborne Diseases

4. Quoted in Ashley Southall, "Cucumbers Recalled in Salmonella Outbreak," *New York Times*, September 5, 2015. www.nytimes.com.
5. Quoted in Kelly Tyko, "Garden Salad Mix Sold at Jewel-Osco, Aldi, Hy-Vee May Be Linked to Cyclospora Outbreak," *USA Today*, June 20, 2020. www.usatoday.com.
6. Quoted in Kelly Tyko, "Salads Recalled from Walmart, Aldi, Hy-Vee, Giant Eagle May Be Linked to Growing Cyclospora Outbreak," *USA Today*, June 27, 2020. www.usatoday.com.

Chapter Two: Waterborne Diseases

7. Quoted in Médecins Sans Frontières, "A Multidisciplinary Approach to Stem the Spread of Cholera," August 21, 2019. www.msf.org.
8. Quoted in Médecins Sans Frontières, "A Multidisciplinary Approach to Stem the Spread of Cholera."
9. Quoted in Médecins Sans Frontières, "A Multidisciplinary Approach to Stem the Spread of Cholera."
10. Quoted in Médecins Sans Frontières, "A Multidisciplinary Approach to Stem the Spread of Cholera."
11. Quoted in World Health Organization, "2.1 Billion People Lack Safe Drinking Water at Home, More than Twice as Many Lack Safe Sanitation," July 12, 2017. www.who.int.
12. Quoted in Tony Barboza, "Disneyland Shuts Down 2 Cooling Towers After Legionnaires' Disease Sickens Park Visitors," *Los Angeles Times*, November 11, 2017. www.latimes.com.
13. Quoted in *Orange County Register* (Anaheim, CA), "Disneyland Cooling Tower Was Likely Source of 2017 Legionnaires' Disease Outbreak, Health Official Testifies," December 6, 2018. www.ocregister.com.

14. Quoted in Deepa Bharath, "Disney Appeals Citation, Penalty over Cooling Towers Potentially Linked with 2017 Legionnaires' Outbreak," *Orange County Register* (Anaheim, CA), September 6, 2018. www.ocregister.com.

Chapter Three: Diseases from Animals and Insects

15. Quoted in Maggie Fox, "Dengue Outbreak Worsens in Hawaii as 139 Ill," NBC News, December 7, 2015. www.nbcnews.com.
16. Quoted in Fox, "Dengue Outbreak Worsens in Hawaii as 139 Ill."
17. Quoted in Coral Beach, "More Victims Anticipated in E. Coli Outbreak Linked to Goat Farm," Food Safety News, March 31, 2016. www.foodsafetynews.com.

Chapter Four: Person-to-Person Infectious Diseases

18. Quoted in World Health Organization, "Intensified Public Health Measures Help Control MERS-CoV Outbreak in the Republic of Korea," July 28, 2015. www.who.int.
19. World Health Organization, "The Public Health Approach to STD Control," 1998. www.who.int.
20. Quoted in Centers for Disease Control and Prevention, "New CDC Report: STDs Continue to Rise in the U.S.," October 8, 2019. www.cdc.gov.
21. Quoted in Kim Krisberg, "Public Health Workers Taking Action on Rising US STD Rates: Gonorrhea, Syphilis Making Comebacks," *Nation's Health*, April 2019. www.thenationshealth.org.
22. Quoted in Central Connecticut Health District, "Department of Public Health Launches #LeaveItToUs Campaign to Reduce Spread of Sexually Transmitted Disease," June 18, 2019. www.ccthd.org.

Chapter Five: Saving Lives with Vaccines

23. Quoted in Pfizer, "Pfizer and BioNTech Announce Vaccine Candidate Against COVID-19 Achieved Success in First Interim Analysis from Phase 3 Study," November 9, 2020. www.pfizer.com.
24. Quoted in US Food and Drug Administration, "FDA Takes Key Action in Fight Against COVID-19 by Issuing Emergency Use Authorization for First COVID-19 Vaccine," December 11, 2020. www.fda.gov.
25. Quoted in Peter Loftus and Melanie Grayce West, "First COVID-19 Vaccine Given to U.S. Public," *Wall Street Journal*, December 14, 2020. www.wsj.com.
26. Quoted in American Pharmacists Association, "Importance of Immunizations to Protect Public Health," February 5, 2015. www.pharmacist.com.
27. Quoted in World Health Organization, "Ebola Vaccine Provides Protection and Hope for High-Risk Communities in the Democratic Republic of the Congo," May 30, 2018. www.who.int.

American Public Health Association (APHA)
www.apha.org

The APHA is the country's leading public health organization and works to advance the health of all people and communities. Its website provides links, news, and other information about a variety of disease topics and research, including infectious diseases.

Centers for Disease Control and Prevention (CDC)
www.cdc.gov

The CDC is the premier public health agency in the United States. Its website includes the latest information about different types of infectious diseases, how they spread, and public health measures to detect and control infectious diseases. Articles and links discuss prevention efforts and public health case studies.

National Foundation for Infectious Diseases (NFID)
www.nfid.org

The NFID is a nonprofit organization that strives to educate health care professionals and the general public about infectious diseases. The NFID website features information about numerous infectious diseases, immunization, and the latest news and reports on infectious disease.

National Institute of Allergy and Infectious Diseases (NIAID)
www.niaid.nih.gov

As part of the National Institutes of Health, the NIAID conducts and supports research to better understand, treat, and prevent infectious and allergic diseases. NIAID research has led to new vaccines, diagnostic tests, and other technologies to improve health for people worldwide. Its website has information and news about infectious diseases, research, vaccines, and more.

US Food and Drug Administration (FDA)
www.fda.gov

The FDA is a federal agency in the US Department of Health and Human Services. It is responsible for protecting public health by ensuring the safety of the US food supply, cosmetics, drugs, and other products. In this role, the FDA often takes part in foodborne and waterborne disease investigations. The FDA website has information and alerts related to foodborne disease.

World Health Organization (WHO)
www.who.int

The WHO is an agency of the United Nations responsible for international public health. The WHO works to promote health for people by conducting research, providing support to local health agencies, and monitoring worldwide health trends, including infectious disease outbreaks. Its website offers information about infectious disease and prevention efforts.

Books

John Allen, *The Origins and Spread of COVID-19*. San Diego, CA: ReferencePoint, 2021.

Michelle Denton, *Pandemics: Deadly Disease Outbreaks*. New York: Lucent, 2020.

Michelle Harris, *Vaccines: The Truth Behind the Debates*. New York: Lucent, 2020.

Erin L. McCoy, *Deadly Viruses*. New York: Cavendish Square, 2019.

Internet Sources

David Adam, "SARS-CoV-2 Isn't Going Away, Experts Predict," The Scientist, January 25, 2021. www.the-scientist.com.

Centers for Disease Control and Prevention, "Innovations to Stop Emerging and Zoonotic Infections," 2017. www.cdc.gov.

Children's Hospital of Philadelphia, "Making Vaccines: How Are Vaccines Made?," 2021. www.chop.edu.

Apoorva Mandavilli, "'The Biggest Monster' Is Spreading. And It's Not the Coronavirus," *New York Times*, August 3, 2020. www.nytimes.com.

Amos Zeeberg, "Piecing Together the Next Pandemic," *New York Times*, February 16, 2021. www.nytimes.com.

INDEX